Other Books by
R.L. STINE

SERIES:

- Goosebumps
- Fear Street
- Rotten School
- Mostly Ghostly

INDIVIDUAL TITLES:

- *It's the First Day of School…Forever!*
- *The Haunting Hour*
- *The Nightmare Hour*
- *The Adventures of Shrinkman*
- *The 13th Warning*
- *The Creatures from Beyond Beyond*
- *Three Faces of Me*
- *My Alien Parents*

ZOMBIE TOWN

Text copyright © 2001 Parachute Press
Cover illustration by Tim Jacobus

A Parachute Press Book

Published by Amazon Publishing
P.O. Box 400818
Las Vegas, NV 89140

ISBN-13: 9781612183299
ISBN-10: 1612183298

R.L. STINE

ZOMBIE TOWN

amazonpublishing

INTRODUCTION

• R.L. STINE •

Do you stay awake nights worrying about zombies? Do you hear sounds outside your window late at night and picture dead people crawling out of their graves and marching...marching and staggering toward your house to grab you, suck out your brain, and eat your flesh?

No. You don't worry about that, and I don't either—most of the time.

But when I was a kid, there was an old graveyard between my house and my school. It would have been faster to walk through the graveyard on my way to school, but I always walked around it. That's because I could picture those rotting bodies coming up from under the ground, just waiting to grab me.

I knew there must be *some* people who think about zombies. There have been hundreds of stories and poems and books and movies and TV shows. And today zombies are more popular than ever.

The living dead are living it up big time! Everywhere you look, the undead are staggering around with their arms stretched out in front of them, drooling for fresh human flesh. Zombies might even be able to win a popularity contest against the all-time horror champions—vampires.

We know that more than two thousand years ago, people wrote poems about the dead returning to life. When they came back, the dead people weren't nice anymore. They were evil—and hungry—just like the zombies we see in movies and on TV.

I've always loved reading books about the tough sailing warriors known as Vikings. In Viking days, there were legends written about living dead people called *Draugrs*. These characters rose up from their graves like wisps of smoke. Then they took human form and grew as large as they wished.

Some Draugrs grew as big as an ox. Being dead didn't make them weak. They had superhuman strength. And according to the legends, they had superhuman *smell*. They stank!

My favorite holiday is Halloween. Did you know that Halloween started because long ago people believed that one day a year at the end of the fall harvest, the spirits would return to walk the earth? On that day, people wore masks so the spirits wouldn't recognize them.

So next Halloween when you put on your mask maybe you want to say thank you to the walking dead. If superstitious people hadn't been so scared of zombies, we wouldn't have any Halloween candy!

The scariest zombies I ever saw were in George A. Romero's film *Night of the Living Dead*. The movie's slogan proclaimed: *They Won't Stay Dead!* The zombies in this film were an army of ghouls—dozens of ugly dead people staggering forward, desperate to grab living humans and eat their brains and their flesh.

Audiences were stunned into silence. There had been scary horror movies for many years, ever since movies were invented. But the hideous, decaying zombies in this film were too real. Adults screamed. Kids cried.

People were upset, but zombies were here to stay. There have been six Living Dead films and dozens of other movies and TV shows in which the dead return to stagger and grunt and satisfy their endless hunger.

A lot of those zombies have staggered their way into *Zombie Town*. I got the idea for this book while sitting in a dark movie theater.

My wife Jane and I live in New York City. One day we went to see a movie in a very big theater. It's an old theater that seats hundreds of people, with a balcony that seats hundreds more.

Jane and I sat down in a middle row and waited for the film to start. We stared at the red curtain that covered the screen, talked, and shared a bucket of popcorn.

After a while, I had a funny feeling. I turned around and realized no one was sitting behind us. I gazed around the whole theater, and I quickly saw that we were the only two people there. This enormous movie theater was empty except for Jane and me.

The doors closed. The lights went down. The theater became very dark. The curtain squeaked as it started to slide open.

I felt a chill at the back of my neck. Being alone in the dark in this huge auditorium was creeping me out. My imagination whirred into overdrive, and I started asking myself scary questions...

Why are we the only ones here? Is this some kind of trap?

What if the doors are locked? What if we're locked in here?

It's too dark and too quiet. Something HORRIFYING is about to happen.

And that's where this book starts. With two kids, Mike and Karen, locked in a dark movie house…and something HORRIFYING is about to happen.

Enjoy.

RL Stine

CHAPTER 1

"See, Mike? Any minute now, it's going to pour," Karen said. "We'll get soaked."

I sat on my front steps and stared up at the sky. Dark clouds rolled low overhead. Thunder rumbled in the distance.

I sighed. Why couldn't it be sunny?

"It's *so* not a good day for skateboarding," Karen said.

"Right," I agreed. "But we *could* hang out and play *Diablo III* on my new laptop."

"We already played it at least a hundred times," she complained. She grabbed my arm. "Come on, Mike! We *have* to do this!"

I sighed again. Karen is my best friend. She lives across the street from me, and we almost always hang out together on Saturdays. Since we couldn't skateboard today, we were trying to decide what to do.

Actually, *I* was the only one trying to decide. Karen already knew.

She wanted to go see *Zombie Town*.

Zombie Town is a horror movie. A terrifying horror movie about a bunch of hideous, flesh-eating zombies who take over a whole town. No one escapes. The zombies eat almost everyone. The survivors get turned into zombies.

Everyone at our school is dying to see *Zombie Town*. Everyone except me.

I hate scary movies. They give me nightmares. They give me *day*mares! It's embarrassing. I mean, I'm twelve. They shouldn't bother me, right? But I can't help it.

"Well?" Karen asked. "Come on, Mike. Let's go check it out!"

"It's going to be really gross, you know," I reminded her. "All those decaying zombies eating people and tearing out their guts."

She laughed. "Cool!"

Cool? Karen *would* say that, I thought. She's not afraid of anything.

"Please, Mike," Karen pleaded. "Don't wimp out on me. Everyone knows there's no such thing as zombies."

I tried to think of other things to do. Help Mr. Bradley next door rake his leaves? No. It would be raining soon. Play with my little brother Zach? Yuck! Go shopping with Mom and Dad? Boring! Clean my room? Was I *that* desperate?

I really, really didn't want to see this movie. But I didn't want to act like a wimp, either. "Okay, I'll go," I finally agreed. "But you buy the popcorn."

"Deal! Meet you at the bus stop in ten minutes!"

Karen ran across the street, and I went inside to tell my parents our plan. I could feel myself getting nervous already. And I hadn't even left my house!

Get a grip, I thought. After all, it *has* been a year since I've seen a scary movie. Maybe now that I'm twelve, I can handle it.

Maybe.

If only I had stayed home…

CHAPTER 2

Half an hour later, Karen and I climbed off the bus at the mall. We ran through the rain to the cineplex across the street. A huge poster hung on the wall outside. It showed a zombie's bloodshot eyes and wide-open mouth. Shreds of human skin dangled from his rotting teeth.

My stomach flip-flopped. "Forget about buying me popcorn," I groaned.

We paid for our tickets. Karen bought herself a giant tub of buttered popcorn. Then we went into the theater.

The place was empty.

"Weird," I said as we walked down the aisle. "This movie is a big hit? Where is everyone?"

"This is excellent." Karen edged into the second row. "We won't have to worry about seeing over somebody's head."

"I guess." Actually, I didn't care if I couldn't see. I didn't *want* to see. Maybe a bunch of seven-foot-tall basketball players would come in and block our view.

A couple of minutes went by. No one came and sat in front of us. Nobody even came into the theater.

I glanced around. All I saw were row after row of empty seats. This isn't just weird, I thought. It's wrong. Something is wrong.

And then I heard it. A low, creaking sound. The creaking grew louder.

I jumped up when I heard a crash. "What was that?" I gasped.

"I see it! A zombie!" Karen screamed. "Run! Run for your life!"

"Where? Where?" I cried.

She laughed. "Chill, Mike. That was the door closing. That's all."

I stared over my shoulder. Karen was right. Someone had closed the door. Now the auditorium was even darker. I sank back into my seat. "We're still the only ones here."

"So what?" Karen asked.

"It doesn't make any sense, that's what!" I cried. "This is the most popular movie in the country. We're all alone in here. Where is everybody?"

"Who cares?" Karen shoved a handful of buttery popcorn into her mouth. "It's cool that nobody's here," she mumbled, chomping down another handful of popcorn. "We have the whole place to ourselves."

I didn't want the whole place to ourselves. I didn't want to be here at all. "I'm getting a really creepy feeling, Karen. I think we..."

"Quiet," she whispered. "It's starting!"

The lights dimmed completely. After a few seconds, some shadowy shapes began moving across the screen. Soft, eerie moaning sounds came from the speakers.

No commercials? I thought. No previews of other movies? What's going on here?

Then I heard voices. Kid's voices.

The screen grew a little brighter. Three kids about my age were walking through a park, laughing and kidding each other. One of them dropped his backpack. Papers and notebooks spilled out. The kids stopped to pick them up.

The moaning grew louder, but the kids didn't notice it. The camera shifted to a grove of bushes behind them.

My heart began to pound.

The bushes rustled. A hand pushed the branches aside. A human hand, with black dirt under long, ragged fingernails.

Black dirt—from the grave.

I cringed as an ugly face peered out from the bushes. Then another one. And another.

The faces had green skin. And one of them had grime all over its nose. Then, as they gazed at the kids, I noticed something.

The nose wasn't grimy. It was missing. The zombie had a gaping black hole in the middle of his face.

It's only make-up, I reminded myself. It's only a movie!

The zombies began to make grunting noises.

Hungry grunting noises.

Karen poked me in the side. "Get ready," she whispered. "They're about to eat their first victims. They have to keep eating people to stay alive, you know."

"Don't remind me," I muttered. I clutched the arms of my seat.

The zombies shoved the bushes aside and staggered into the open. The camera closed in on the noseless zombie's face.

As he gazed hungrily at the kids, one of his eyeballs slid out of the socket.

My stomach flipped over. Oh, man! I thought. Why did I ever let Karen talk me into this?

On the screen, the kids turned their heads. Their eyes grew wide with horror. The zombies loomed over them, moaning and smacking their rotted, swollen lips.

I knew what was coming. And I didn't want to see it. As the kids screamed in terror, I squeezed my eyes shut.

A piercing shriek rang out.

I started to cover my ears, but the shriek suddenly stopped. Then I heard a sputtering noise, sort of like a piece of plastic fluttering in the wind.

I opened my eyes, just a slit.

Huh? The screen had gone dark.

I glanced around.

Except for the dim red glow of the exit sign, the theater was dark.

Dark and totally silent.

CHAPTER 3

"I don't believe it!" Karen cried.

"What?" I asked. "What's going on?"

"Didn't you hear that sputtering sound?" she replied. "It was the film flapping around. The projector broke."

"Oh. Too bad," I lied. Secretly, I felt relieved. Now I wouldn't have to see the rest of the film. "I guess we'd better go."

"No way. The movie just started," Karen declared. "They'll fix it. Just wait."

Karen leaned back in her seat and chomped on her popcorn. I kept my fingers crossed that somebody would announce that the film had been ripped to shreds.

A couple of minutes went by.

"Hey, projectionist!" Karen shouted. "How long until the movie starts again?"

No answer.

We swiveled around in our seats and glanced up at the projection booth above the balcony. The booth was empty.

Just like the theater.

Karen stood up. "The projectionist must be out in the lobby. Let's go see."

We stumbled up the aisle to the door. I pushed on the bar.

The door didn't open. I pushed harder. No. It still wouldn't open. "It's stuck," I groaned.

Karen leaned her shoulder against the door and shoved. I pushed on the bar.

The door didn't budge.

"It's not stuck—it's locked!" I cried. I pounded on it with my fists. "Hey, somebody—we're locked in here! Let us out!"

We waited for a few seconds. Nothing happened. I pounded and shouted again, but no one came.

"This is so not cool," Karen declared.

"Yeah." I turned and gazed at the rows of empty seats. My heart started to thud, and my mouth felt dry. "Why isn't someone opening the door?"

"I don't know." Karen glanced around. "But we're not stuck, Mike. We can get out through the emergency door." She pointed down the aisle.

I gazed at the glowing red exit sign. Yes! The sooner we got out of here, the better.

As we hurried down the sloping aisle, Karen tripped on the leg of a seat. Her tub of popcorn flew out of her hand. Popcorn rolled down the aisle like an avalanche.

"There goes four dollars down the drain," she griped. "Down the aisle, I mean! I'm going to ask for a free refill."

"Who's going to give it to you?" I asked. "There isn't anyone here!"

"Somebody has to be around," she argued. "They probably all took a break at the same time or something."

Maybe she's right, I thought. But I didn't care. Once we got out, I was going home. Karen could stay and watch the movie alone. Let her call me a wimp.

We reached the bottom of the aisle. I stepped up to the emergency door—and pushed hard with both hands.

Nothing happened.

Karen joined me. We both pushed. Then we tried pulling.

The door didn't move.

My heart began to pound again. We're trapped in here, I realized.

Someone locked us in. But—why?

CHAPTER 4

"Wh-what are we going to do?" I stammered. My legs were shaking. I dropped into the nearest seat.

"Don't panic," Karen said. "It's no big deal. Really." She swallowed hard. "Well…maybe it *is* a little creepy."

"No kidding." I leaned against the seat back and stared around. I couldn't see anything but the shadows of the empty seats. I couldn't hear anything but my heart pounding.

"Hellooo!" Karen suddenly shouted. "We're stuck in here! If this is a joke, we're not laughing! Let us out!"

No one answered. When Karen's voice stopped echoing, the theater grew silent again.

We have to get out of here, I thought. There has to be a way! I glanced up at the blank movie screen. "Let's go back there, behind the screen," I suggested. "Maybe there's another emergency door."

Maybe even a telephone, I thought. I was definitely ready to dial 911.

We hopped onto the dusty stage and pulled back one end of the screen. As we stepped behind it, a disgusting, putrid smell swept over us.

"Whoa, gross!" Karen exclaimed. "What *is* that?"

I clapped my hands over my mouth and nose. "I don't know," I mumbled. "Rotten eggs, maybe?"

"Eeew! I think I'm going to be sick," Karen groaned. Her face turned green.

"Hold it until we get outside. Look!" I pointed across the stage to a door with another red EXIT sign above it.

"Great!" Karen cried. "Let's get out of here before I puke."

We started toward the door. But halfway across the stage, I heard something.

A shuffling noise, like someone's feet scraping across the dusty wood floor. Then I heard a soft wheezing sound. In and out. In and out.

I grabbed Karen's arm. The shuffling noise came again. "Did you hear that?" I asked.

"It's probably the screen moving back and forth." She tried to tug her arm free.

"No, wait. There's something else. Listen!" I whispered.

Karen gave me an annoyed glance. She started to say something, but I held up my hand to silence her.

In the silence, I heard the wheezing again. In and out. Getting louder. Louder.

"Unnh…unnnnh!"

My skin prickled.

Karen's eyes grew wide. "What is that?" she whispered.

I shook my head.

"Unnnnh!" The frightening sound came closer. We heard the shuffling again.

Then a figure slowly emerged from the shadows near the door. The eerie red glow of the exit sign lit up his face.

"Noooooooo!" Karen moaned.

My teeth started to chatter. I couldn't speak.

A zombie stared at us from across the stage.

A zombie, with green skin and a haunted, hungry look in his eyes.

No, not his eyes. His *eye*! One eye was missing. And as the living corpse turned, I could see that half his face was missing, too. As if someone had ripped off the skin on his right side.

"Karen!" I gasped. "It's—it's—a zombie from the movie!"

"His mouth! Look at his mouth!" she cried.

"Huh?"

"See what's stuck in his teeth?"

I forced myself to stare into the zombie's mouth. Something silver glittered between two rotting teeth.

A buckle.

I had seen that buckle before. In the movie. On the backpack the kid had dropped right before the zombies attacked.

That buckle—was that all that was left of the kid?

Did the zombie eat the rest of him?

But that was a movie! I told myself. It wasn't real! It couldn't be!

My knees started to shake again. Chill after chill ran down my back.

The zombie's one eye slipped out of its socket and rested on its cheekbone.

The ugly creature let out a loud moan. Karen and I jumped back, screaming.

The zombie lifted his head. The eye locked on us. Then the creature raised half-rotted arms and took a lurching step. "Unnnh...unnnnnh!"

"Karen...Karen..." I whispered. "It's coming after us!"

CHAPTER 5

Karen froze beside me.

I wanted to run. But my legs wouldn't cooperate.

The sour smell surrounded us.

The silver buckle glittered in the zombie's crooked teeth.

I yanked on Karen's arm. "Come on!" I shouted. "Remember what you said? They have to keep eating people to stay alive. You see any other people around here besides us?"

"I can't believe this," Karen murmured. "It's unreal."

The zombie took another shuffling step and moaned again. A low, hungry moan.

"Is that real enough for you?" I demanded.

Karen grabbed my hand. Together, we finally got moving. We raced around in front of the screen.

I glanced back over my shoulder. The zombie was still behind the screen, but I could hear it moaning and shuffling along.

"No such things as zombies, huh?" I whispered to Karen.

"I don't get it!" Karen cried. "I just don't get it. How could that thing actually get out of a movie?"

"I don't know!" I said as we leaped off the stage. "But it's out. And it's after us."

The zombie moaned again. "At least they don't move fast," Karen told me. "We can beat it out of here easy!"

"Out of here?" I suddenly remembered something. "The doors are locked!"

Karen stared at me. For the first time, she looked really terrified. "I...I forgot about that!"

I turned at the sound of another moan. The movie screen rippled and shook. Then, as I gaped in horror, a long slit appeared down the middle. The zombie ripped it wide open!

As his face peered out, searching the darkness for us, Karen and I both shrieked.

"We can't just stand here!" I shouted. "We have to try the door again. Come on!" We started to race up the aisle.

And stopped, screaming in terror.

Another zombie waited for us at the top of the aisle.

A zombie with a dark hole where its nose should have been.

A third one crawled over the seats on the right, grabbing at the cushions with blackened fingernails.

"No. No." Karen gasped.

"The movie!" I cried. "All three of them escaped from the movie!"

Karen grabbed my arm. "Count again, Mike," she whispered.

I turned to see a fourth zombie with bloodshot eyes crawl across the seats on the left. A human hand dangled from its teeth.

Loud, hungry moans echoed from behind us. We spun around and gasped.

The zombie with the missing eye stood at the front of the stage.

But it wasn't alone anymore.

At least ten more zombies had joined it.

Ten more hungry zombies, I thought, my mind spinning in terror. Zombies who need human flesh to stay alive.

Our flesh!

We bolted to the first exit door and rammed our shoulders against it.

Still locked.

We flew up the side aisle to the back door.

It still wouldn't open.

"Unnh! Unnnnh!" The zombies jumped down from the stage. They came after us, slithering, groaning, staggering.

It doesn't matter how slow they are, I realized. We can't escape. We can run around in here for hours, but they'll still catch us.

I stared in horror at the hand—someone's hand!—hanging from the zombie's mouth.

They'll catch us, I knew.

And then they'll eat us.

CHAPTER 6

There has to be another way out of here, I thought desperately. As I glanced all around, I suddenly remembered.

"The balcony!" I shouted. "Come on!"

I grabbed Karen's hand and pulled her along until we found the balcony stairs. We stumbled up the steps to the very top.

Black velvet curtains covered the back wall.

Just curtains. No door.

Below us, the zombies moaned and wailed.

I spun around and peered down. I could see them lumbering toward the balcony stairs. Then they disappeared from sight.

A couple of seconds passed. Then I heard their footsteps. Heavy. Thudding. Climbing up the steps.

Karen yanked on my sleeve. "The projection booth!"

We scurried along the back wall to the little glass-fronted booth. I grabbed hold of the door handle and turned it.

The handle broke off.

I heard the zombies climbing. Getting closer. Moaning for food. *Human* food.

I rammed my shoulder against the door. The door rattled and shook, but it didn't open.

Karen screamed. I stumbled back and fell to the floor. She screamed again, pointing.

A zombie stood at the top of the stairs. Its lips hung open. As it grinned at us, I could see the fuzzy black mold that covered its teeth.

More zombies crowded behind it. They gazed at us hungrily, grunting, sniffing.

Then they began to stagger toward us.

"Oh, man, oh, man!" My legs turned to mush. My whole body shook. "There's no place to go! We're cornered!"

"Trapped…" Karen muttered. "We're trapped…"

CHAPTER 7

The zombies pressed forward. Lurching stiffly, their hungry eyes locked on us. Their sick, sour smell surrounded us. They groaned and grunted, deep, throaty moans of the living dead.

Panic choked my throat. My hands were squeezed into tight fists. I glanced down and saw that I still had the door handle in my hand.

I don't know where I got the courage. I didn't even think about it. It just sort of happened.

As the one with the moldy teeth drew closer, I swung my arm back—and flung the door handle into his face.

The handle made a sick, squishy sound as it hit. A piece of green skin ripped off.

"Yaiiii!" The zombie let out a squeal and grabbed his torn cheek.

The others joined in, howling in anger, their bodies moving excitedly up and down like puppets.

"What did you do?" Karen shrieked. "You—you made them even angrier!"

"What difference does it make?" I yelled. "They're going to get us anyway!"

The snarling, howling zombies staggered closer.

Karen and I stepped back. We hit the back wall. Nowhere to run.

This is it! I thought in horror, as I felt the velvet curtains behind me. This is as far as we can go.

We pressed ourselves into the thick curtains. I closed my eyes. The zombie smell sickened me. Their horrifying moans rang in my ears.

I heard a loud click.

And the wall gave way!

"Whoaaa!" I cried out as Karen and I fell backwards. We thudded to the floor in a tangle of velvet curtains.

"A door!" Karen cried, struggling to untangle herself from the curtains. She scrambled to her feet. "Another emergency door!"

I glanced back through the open door. A zombie stared back at me with one eye. A trail of yellow slime oozed from its other eye socket.

The other zombies crowded behind it.

Karen and I took off, racing down the stairs to the lobby.

Please, let the front doors open! I thought as we stumbled across the slick lobby floor. Please!

We slammed against the metal bars—and the doors flew open!

As we burst out onto the sidewalk, Karen slipped in a rain puddle. She landed hard on her hands and knees.

"Get up! Hurry!" I took hold of her arm and tried to pull her up.

Karen glanced over her shoulder at the theater.

"Hurry!" I repeated.

Karen finally stood up. But she didn't move. She kept gazing at the theater with a frown on her face.

"What are you waiting for?" I shrieked.

"Nothing. I'm thinking," she told me.

"Oh, great! Why don't you think about getting out of here?" I took her arm again and tugged her across the street.

"I'm not so sure we have to hurry." Karen pointed to the theater. "Look, Mike. The lobby is still empty."

"So what? The zombies are slow, remember?"

"Not that slow." Karen stared at the theater. Then at me. Then she burst out laughing.

"Are you nuts?" I hollered. "What are you laughing about?"

"The zombies!" she exclaimed. "I figured it out, Mike!"

"Huh?"

"I figured it all out," Karen said.

CHAPTER 8

"I knew it couldn't be real," she declared. "The whole thing was a trick. Some kind of publicity stunt for the movie. The zombies were fakes."

"But...but I smelled them!" I stammered. "I'll never forget that smell. You saw how real they were."

"Costumes," she told me. "Costumes sprayed with a disgusting smell, that's all." She pointed across the street to the theater again. "The lobby is still empty, see?"

I stared through the glass doors. Karen was right.

"If the zombies were real, they would have been downstairs by now," Karen declared.

"But what about the locked doors?" I demanded. "And why were we the only ones in the place? What happened to the ticket-seller and the pop-corn guy?"

"All that was part of the stunt, I guess. It had to be," Karen insisted. "I mean, everybody knows there's no such thing as zombies."

I kept staring into the lobby. No zombies appeared. Was Karen right?

"That was so cool." Karen laughed again. "I was scared out of my mind. They really fooled us, didn't they?"

I didn't know what to believe. The zombies seemed so real! My heart still raced and my hands were still shaking. All I wanted to do was get home, fast.

I glanced down the street. Good. The bus was only two blocks away. The sooner I got away from here, the better.

The bus rumbled toward us. It bounced through a pothole and swerved to the side, almost hitting a lamppost.

"Whoa!" Karen cried. "That thing's really flying!"

The tires squealed as the bus swerved back to the middle of the street. I waved my arms, but the driver didn't slow down. He blasted the horn, then gripped the wheel with both hands and kept speeding toward us.

The bus zoomed closer. The engine roared. The bus jolted over another pothole and swerved again.

The headlights swept over us. I gaped in horror.

"Karen—jump!" I screamed. "It's going to hit us!"

CHAPTER 9

I grabbed Karen. Leaped back from the curb. And threw myself against the brick wall of the store behind us.

The horn blared. Tires squealed. A fountain of water splashed from the gutter as the bus shot past us in a blur.

We were drenched. I wiped my eyes and stared after the bus as it squealed around a corner. "What's the matter with that guy?" I sputtered. "He's nuts!"

"Maybe the gas pedal got stuck or something." Karen shook her head, spattering me with water. "I guess we'll have to walk home instead."

"Forget it," I told her. "I'm wet and cold. Let's call my mom for a ride."

"You're still worried about the zombies, aren't you?" Karen teased. "Check out the lobby, Mike. Nobody's there."

"Okay, okay." She was right, but I didn't care. "I still don't want to walk. Come on, let's find a pay phone."

Our sneakers squished as we walked toward a Kwikee-Mart in the middle of the next block. The rain had stopped, but it didn't matter—both of us were soaked.

I kept glancing over my shoulder, checking for zombies. Karen laughed every time I did. But I couldn't help it. The whole stunt had really frightened me.

If it *was* a stunt.

We squished into the Kwikee-Mart and found the pay phone near the front counter. While Karen checked out the magazine rack, I dropped a quarter in and punched my phone number. Then I glanced around the store.

The place was empty. I craned my neck and stared at the front counter. No one there. Where was the owner?

I let the phone ring ten times...twenty. I hung up and checked the clock over the counter. Five-thirty. Mom and Dad should both be home. I got my quarter back and tried again.

Still no answer.

I tried Karen's house next. While I listened to the phone ring, I noticed something.

The cash register drawer stood open. A couple of the little compartments were empty. But a few tens and even some twenties were left.

I frowned. Why would the owner leave the drawer open? Maybe the place had been robbed, and he ran to the police. But wait a second. Why didn't the robber take all the money?

The phone kept ringing. No answer at Karen's house, either.

When I hung up, I heard a whirring sound.

"Hey, Mike, come here," Karen called. "Check this out."

I crossed to the other side of the store. The whirring grew louder.

Karen stood in front of the Slushy Machine. Its motor was running, churning out cherry slush. The slush had overflowed the cup underneath. Now it spread across the counter and plopped onto the floor in big red globs.

I glanced around the empty store again and frowned.

What was going on?

Where was everyone? What was happening here? Where had they all gone?

CHAPTER 10

"Weird, huh?" Karen whispered, watching the cherry slush plop onto the floor.

"Yeah. That's not the only thing that's weird," I told her. "Check out the cash register. It's wide open."

"Whoa. I don't believe it!" she said. "This is very creepy."

"No kidding. Let's go," I told her. "Nobody's home at my place. Or yours, either. We'll have to walk."

When we left the Kwikee-Mart, I checked up and down the street.

"Stop looking for zombies. You're making me nervous." Karen said. "It had to be a stunt, Mike. Zombies don't exist—not in real life."

"Maybe. Maybe not," I said. "But I have this prickly feeling on the back of my neck, like something's crawling on it."

Karen shivered. "Are you sure no one answered the phone at my house?" she asked. "Dad's supposed to be watching a football game. And Mom told me she was going to grade papers all afternoon."

"My parents are supposed to be home, too," I said. I took another quick look behind me. Nothing. "All I know is, I let both phones ring about a hundred times."

"Maybe they all changed their minds and decided to go out," Karen suggested. "It *is* Saturday."

"So how come the sidewalks are empty?" I asked. "Where are all the people?"

"*There's* someone!" Karen pointed behind us. I turned to look.

A car sped up the street. As it zoomed past, I saw a man and a woman jammed inside with piles of clothes, a rocking chair, and a television set.

The car squealed around the corner and flew onto the highway leading out of town.

Behind it came a pick-up truck with five kids in the back. The kids hung on tight as the truck skidded around the corner and sped toward the highway.

"Those people are going to get speeding tickets," Karen declared.

"Yeah. But I don't see any police cars around," I told her. "Except for that one."

I pointed at the blue car parked at the curb. Actually, it wasn't exactly parked. Its front wheels sat on the sidewalk. Its rear end stuck out into the street.

Other cars had been parked at weird angles, too. The radio in one of them blared loudly through the open driver's-side door.

The cars looked as if they had been parked in a hurry—and then abandoned.

That crawly feeling on the back of my neck grew stronger. "What is going on around here?" I asked. I waved my arm. "Look at all the houses."

We had entered the neighborhood where we live, and the front door of almost every house stood wide open. They swung back and forth in the wind, and slapped against the houses.

No one came to close them.

A leaf blower lay in a yard, buzzing noisily.

No one came to turn it off.

A dirt bike lay at the end of a driveway with its engine sputtering. Black smoke spewed into the air.

No one came to check it out.

"See what I mean?" I said. "Nobody is around."

"Yeah. And it's like they all left in a hurry," Karen agreed.

I felt a chill roll down my back. I saw Karen's chin tremble.

That made me even *more* nervous. After all, I'm the one who gets scared and has nightmares. Not Karen. If she's scared, then something is seriously wrong.

I checked over my shoulder again. No zombies. But no people, either.

We hurried across the street to the next block. The houses looked the same—deserted. As we turned the corner onto our block, we began to run.

"Don't worry!" Karen gasped. "There has to be *some* explanation!"

Sure, I thought. But what?

CHAPTER 11

We split up when we reached the middle of our block. Karen ran to her house, and I dashed across the street to mine.

Our minivan stood in the driveway. The front door of the house was closed. Alright! I thought. Mom and Dad are home. Now I'll find out what's happening.

I banged through the door and stumbled into the hall. "Mom! Dad!" I shouted. "I'm home! And something really spooky is going on outside!"

I paused to catch my breath. Why is it so dark in here? I wondered. The hallway light was off. *All the lights were off.*

"Hello! Mom?" I hollered. "Dad? Zach?"

My voice echoed in the front hall.

But no one answered.

My heart skipped a beat. I froze, suddenly cold all over.

They have to be home, I thought. The van is here.

I jumped when I heard a voice. From the den at the back of the house.

The television! That's where they are, I thought. They're all watching TV in the den.

I hurried down the hall and peered around the door.

The den lights were off, too. The only light came from the TV. It flickered on the wall, casting weird shadows around the room.

My parents and Zach sat on the couch. Zipper, my dog, curled on the floor in front of them.

A man on the TV held up a bottle of pills. "Folks, try the Extra-Energy Vitamin tablets and give your life a boost!" he boomed. "In ten days, I guarantee you'll have more bounce in those bones than in the past ten years!"

I frowned. An infomercial?

Mom and Dad never watch those things. And Zach only likes cartoons.

"Hey, I'm home," I declared. "How come you're all sitting around in the dark?"

I reached around the door and flipped on the light.

And opened my mouth in a scream of horror.

CHAPTER 12

I gaped at my dad. At his sunken eyes, his slack jaw. The green skin sagging from his face.

My mom's eyes drooped from their sockets, hanging by veiny threads. Her lips were fat and swollen. A chunk of her hair lay in her lap. I could see some of her skull through the wide bald spot in her head.

Zach stared blankly at me. His mouth hung open. His teeth were gone. His nose dripped dark yellow pus. A patch of skin had fallen from his cheek, and a jagged bone poked through.

Zipper's fur had fallen off. His skin was as green as everyone else's.

Zombies. All zombies.

I squeezed my eyes shut and shook my head. It can't be true! I told myself. They're wearing make-up. They sprayed themselves green. It has to be a joke. A really sick joke.

"Hey, you guys, this isn't funny," I choked out.

No one answered.

Then Dad slowly lifted his hand and scratched his ear.

"Ohhh!" I uttered a cry as the ear fell off!

Dad moaned. He picked up the ear from his lap in green, bony fingers and stared at it blankly for a second. Then he tossed the ear to Zipper, who wolfed it down hungrily.

My heart drummed in my chest. My mouth went dry and my legs trembled.

This is no joke! I realized. There *are* such things as zombies! Somehow, *Zombie Town* has become real!

And I was living in it!

That's why the bus and the cars had been going so fast. They were trying to escape.

That's why the Kwikee-Mart was empty. The owner abandoned it. He didn't even take time to grab all his money.

That explained the empty houses with their doors flung open. The deserted cars. The abandoned dirt bike and leaf blower.

Everyone had run. Run for their lives. Because the zombies were taking over the town!

But not everyone made it out, I realized. Some of them must have been eaten.

And some of them became zombies.

Like my family.

Zipper suddenly snarled, snapping me out of my terrifying thoughts.

I stared down at him. Blue-green mold already covered the dog's teeth, but they still appeared sharp. And those sharp teeth were clamped around a bone.

A long, thick bone, with chunks of flesh still dangling from it.

My stomach flipped over. Was that a *human* bone?

Snarling hungrily, Zipper held the bone down with one paw He ripped off a fat chunk of flesh and sucked it into his mouth.

My stomach lurched.

Zipper growled.

Mom and Dad and Zach turned their heads and stared at me, as if seeing me for the first time.

Slowly, the three of them rose from the couch. Zipper lumbered to his feet.

Mom raised a bony hand toward me. Reaching for me. Her swollen lips rippled. "Unnnnh!" she moaned.

"Unnh! Unnnnh!" Dad and Zach began moaning, too.

Zipper growled.

Then all four of them began staggering toward me, moaning with hunger.

CHAPTER 13

"No!" I screamed. I didn't want to believe it, but it was true—my own family was coming after me!

They were zombies now. Hungry, flesh-eating zombies.

And they wanted to eat *me*!

"Nooo!" I screamed again. Then I forced myself to move. I spun away from them and tore down the hall to the front door.

I flew outside and skidded on the wet front porch. I somersaulted down the steps and hit the sidewalk with a thud, flat on my back.

"Unnnh!" I heard a zombie moaning close by. Too close.

Zombies can't move that fast, I thought. It couldn't be Mom and Dad, not yet anyway.

I leaped to my feet and glanced around.

Mr. Bradley stood in his yard next door, gazing at me across the hedge. His sagging skin was a dull green. His sunken eyes glowed with hunger.

"They're all zombies!" I screamed. I sprinted down the sidewalk.

As I raced into the street, I saw a crowd of zombies lurching toward me. The one in front had an empty eye socket oozing with yellow slime.

I blinked. I recognized them. The zombies from the movie!

"Karen!" I screamed. I raced across the street toward her house. "The zombies are taking over the town. We have to get out!"

I leaped onto her porch and burst through the front door. "Karen!" I shouted. "Karen!"

Karen stepped out from one of the rooms. She stood at the end of the hall, gazing at me.

"Unnh!" she groaned and licked her lips. Patches of green mold had already started growing on her face. Drool spilled out of her torn mouth. She moaned again. "Unnnnnh!"

I raced back to the front door.

Mr. Bradley lumbered onto the porch. Behind him came my family. Zipper staggered ahead of them, growling. The movie zombies lurched up the sidewalk.

I spun around. Karen still stood at the end of the hall, blocking the back door.

I heard a thump—and whirled around. Mr. Bradley's arm had dropped off. He howled and kept staggering toward the door. Zipper lunged for the arm with an evil, vicious snarl.

"Unnnnh!" Karen moaned. She took a heavy, plodding step toward me. Another. Another.

The zombies shuffled across the porch, crowding around the front door.

I dove into the hall and tumbled into the living room. I hopped to my feet and ran through the archway into the dining room. As I raced around the table, I grabbed bananas and apples from the fruit bowl and scattered them behind me.

Maybe it will slow them down, I thought. Maybe they'll slip and fall. They won't eat the fruit, of course. They need flesh. *My* flesh.

I slammed through another door and skidded to a stop in the kitchen. I glanced around, gasping for breath.

The only door in the kitchen led back to the hall. To Karen. There was no chance for escape that way.

I could hear the zombies shuffling heavily through the living room. I couldn't get out that way, either!

Shaking with terror, I climbed into the sink and tried to open the window above it. The window slid up an inch.

Then it stuck!

I pounded on the frame, then tried to lift it again. And again.

The window wouldn't budge.

"Unnh. Unnnnhhh!" The zombies moaned and grunted. Louder. Closer. They were in the dining room now!

Footsteps shuffled outside the door to the hall. A shadow fell across the kitchen floor.

Karen!

I dropped to the floor and pulled open the cabinet underneath the sink. In a panic, I yanked out soap and sponges, cans of sink scrubber and window cleaner. Then I tried to crawl inside.

I didn't fit! My legs stuck out. I couldn't close the cabinet doors!

A zombie lurched through the dining room door.

Karen staggered in through the hall.

They've got me, I thought.

I tried to make myself smaller, to squeeze farther into the cabinet. But I was trapped and I knew it.

I'm doomed, I realized. Doomed...

I shut my eyes and waited for them to grab me.

CHAPTER 14

The movie screen went dark. The overhead lights came on in a small, private screening room.

Martin McNair, the famous director of horror movies, rose from his seat and faced a group of twenty-five kids.

The kids all clapped and cheered. McNair smiled. "Thanks for coming," he told them. "As a director, I like to get an audience's opinion before the movie opens. So I thank you for coming to see this sneak preview of my new movie, *Zombie Town*. You were a great audience."

The kids clapped some more. "So, what did you think of it?" McNair asked.

"It was awesome," a boy declared. "Especially the dog. I loved the way he chomped up that human bone."

"The special effects were really cool," another boy chimed in. "Karen looked really creepy when she became a zombie."

"But *why* did she have to turn into a zombie at the end?" a girl asked. "I really liked her."

"And I think Mike should have escaped," a boy said.

"You do? Why?" the director asked.

The boy shrugged. "I don't know. I guess because he and Karen were supposed to be the heroes, and they lost. There was nobody left but zombies."

"Who cares?" The girl sitting next to him snorted. "Does every story have to have a happy ending? Besides, everyone knows there's no such thing as zombies."

She heard a cough and turned around. She stared at the weird-looking people who jammed the back row. Their eyes were deep in their sockets. Their patchy skin was green and decayed. Gray bone showed through their scalps. Some had missing ears and noses.

"Hey—!" the girl cried. "They're not real, are they? There's no such thing as zombies, right? RIGHT?"

ABOUT THE AUTHOR

Photograph © Dan Nelken

R.L. (Robert Lawrence) Stine is one of the best-selling children's authors in history. His Goosebumps series, along with such series as Fear Street, The Nightmare Room, Rotten School, and Mostly Ghostly have sold nearly 400 million books in this country alone. And they are translated into 32 languages.

The *Goosebumps* TV series was the top-rated kids' series for three years in a row. R.L.'s TV movies, including *The Haunting Hour: Don't Think About It* and *Mostly Ghostly*, are perennial Halloween favorites. And his scary TV series, *R.L. Stine's The Haunting Hour*, is in its second season on The Hub network.

R.L. continues to turn out Goosebumps books, published by Scholastic. In addition, his first horror novel for adults in many years, titled *Red Rain*, will be published by Touchstone books in October 2012.

R.L. says that he enjoys his job of "scaring kids." But the biggest thrill for him is turning kids on to reading.

R.L. lives in New York City with his wife, Jane, an editor and publisher, and King Charles Spaniel, Minnie. His son, Matthew, is a sound designer and music producer.